I Am The Streets

Book 3

T.L. Joy

Table of Contents

Chapter One

"Just hang on 'Tiva.... Once you get out of this shit it's gonna be all good," Gunz spoke through the phone. Since I'd been locked up in this bitch, the only person I could talk to was Gunz. He was the only one from the outside world to keep me sane, and for that, I appreciated him.

"I know..." I sighed. "How's everything goin'? Any word on 'Tya?" I asked.

"Everything gucci ova' here. As far as 'Tya, it seems like she disappeared out of thin air."

"Disappeared?" I scrunched my face up in confusion. "What the fuck you mean she disappeared?"

"We haven't seen any activity from her. The club is still running, but your manager been running it.

So it seem like 'Tya been real low key," he explained. I could feel my blood boil from anger.

"Aiight. Keep me posted when you find her," I replied.

"Fa'sho, but you stay up 'Tiva. I'll catch up with you next time we talk," Gunz said as the operator began telling us that our call was coming down to one minute left.

"Aiight. I'll holla at you later," I said before hanging up the phone.

I glanced around the hallways as I was escorted by the correctional officer back to my cell. It's been exactly a year of being locked up and I had seen so much shit happen since I was in here. I'd seen bitches fighting, raping, and killing, all over some stupid shit. Some would try to befriend you and then fuck you over on some sneak shit. It didn't take long for me to catch on. I quickly learned the first, basic rule of the inside was that I couldn't trust nobody in this bitch. I stayed to myself and played my damn role. I had a fuckin' ten-year bid for drug and sex trafficking and I'd be damned if I let these dumb bitches kill me before I could even see the outside again.

As soon as I got back to my cell, I laid onto my bunk bed and began reading The 48 Laws of Power to help time pass. That was all I could do while I was stuck in this shitty ass cell. I watched as my cell mate finally walked into our cell.

She was 5'8" with smooth chocolate skin, a big-boned build, and a bald head with tattoos on the side of her face. Yet none of that shit intimidated me. She'd been my cell mate for the past six months and we hadn't had one problem. Once she found out who I was, we gained a mutual respect.

Our eyes connected when she walked into the cell and she gave a quick head nod to say wassup. I returned the nod and went back to reading until the guard yelled out.

"Lights out!"

I slid my book under my pillow and looked up at the ceiling as the lights shut off. My mind paced and I began reflecting on my life. How did I come from being a prissy-ass career woman, living the high life, to this? Here I was locked up with a bitch name Killa' doing a ten-year bid on some shit that my own flesh and blood pinned on me. I shook my head in disgust as I rolled over and went to sleep. Shit couldn't get no worse than this!

~~~

"Get up Inmate 8741! Get up!" the guard yelled out, causing me to jolt out of my sleep.

I rubbed my aching eyes and zoned in on the tall female officer standing in front of my cell. It still was dark in the jail so it had to be late, past midnight. *What the fuck they want with me?*

I slid out of my bunk and headed over to the bars. "Wha-what's going on?" I asked groggily.

"Don't ask no fuckin' questions. Come with me," she commanded as she opened up my cell and handcuffed me.

I stepped out the cell and followed her down the hall in pure confusion. I looked around and saw that all the other inmates were sleeping soundly in their cells while this officer led me deeper and deeper into the prison. I started to notice that the area we were in was old and clearly under construction. Then there wasn't even a security camera in sight. Stopping in my tracks, I called out to the officer.

"Who the fuck sent you?" I spat.

The female officer stopped with her back still to me and let out a low chuckle. She slowly spun around with a wild grin on her face. "The Reaper sent his regards," she disclosed before rushing toward me. With her nightstick in hand, she cracked the metal baton against my head. Tumbling to the floor, I laid there looking up in horror as the female officer bared down on me swinging her nightstick like she was a batter trying to hit a home run.

With no way to defend myself I was at the female officer's will. I winced as I heard a loud crack and a rush of pain surging from my rib cage. Dropping the nightstick, the officer hoisted me up to my feet and threw me against the wall. Hitting the wall with a thud, I screamed out in agony. Trying to gain my balance on the wall, I looked and saw the female officer running at me with a sharp object in her hand. With three quick thrust she stabbed me in the stomach. Blood oozed from my wounds as I slid down the wall and onto my face. The female officer suddenly took off, believing that she had finished her job. But there I lay struggling to breathe when I heard footsteps running toward where I was. *I just have to hold on,* I thought to myself before everything went black.

When I came back to consciousness, I was blinded by white fluorescent lights and a doctor scurrying around the room. I opened my mouth to say something but my voice was muffled. The doctor turned around and walked over to me.

"Everything is going to be ok, ma'am, just breathe slowly," he instructed as he held the oxygen mask over my face. I nodded my head and took in the air gratefully before passing back out.

Even though I laid in the hospital bed in critical condition, it was by the grace of God that I survived. Because of what happened, it was decided that I would be transferred to another prison under high security. I was in so much pain that I could barely close my eyes. All my problems from the outside were now trying to get me from inside the prison walls. I'd only been here for one year, and now I had to try to stay alive for nine more.

Chapter Two

Today was the day. As I stepped outside, I could feel the warm sun shining on me. I couldn't help but smile as I stepped out on the other side of the barbed wire gate. I was finally getting my chance of freedom. With good behavior and not having a previous criminal record before this, I was able to get out after serving three years in state prison.

There standing in front of his matte black Range Rover was the one person I had left in the world...Gunz. I didn't have any friends or family to come get me. Instead I had the one person who felt they owed their life to me since I saved him from meeting his maker.

"I'm outta this bitch!" I screeched as I rushed over and embraced Gunz out of excitement.

"Welcome back ma!" He smiled and looked at me after we broke our long hug. Never in my life had I been so happy to see someone who I wasn't even fuckin' or had a love connection with.

"We got a lot to catch up on..." He glanced back at the officer stationed at the gate entrance. "You ready to go?" he asked.

"Hell yeah! I been ready!" I exclaimed.

Gunz chuckled. "Aiight, let's roll then."

Without another word said, he opened the passenger door and helped me get in his car sitting high up off the ground. Lantana's "All Hustle, No Luck" blasted through his sound system as we drove off onto the freeway.

"So where are we going?" I looked over to him.

"There is someone who wants to meet you so we have to make that stop first," he answered as his eyes never left the road.

"Who the fuck wants to meet me?" I snapped, only to be met with Gunz's laughter.

"Yo' ass is crazy girl." He looked over at me and smirked.

"But foreal though, the connect wants to meet you," Gunz revealed.

"The connect huh? I finally get to meet him," I thought aloud.

"It's been long enough." He shrugged.

"You got that right." I nodded.

"Anything I need to know about him before I get there?" I inquired.

"Nah, you good ma. Just stay calm 'n' cool like how you normally be, and it won't be no problems," Gunz disclosed.

"Aiight...we'll see how this go," was all I said before I looked out the window and slowly began to doze off.

By the time I opened my eyes, we were parked in front of a large estate that appeared to be in the middle of nowhere.

"We here..." Gunz announced as I rubbed my eyes and looked around the highly wooded area.

"C'mon, let's go," he continued before hopping out of the parked car. I quickly regained my composure and hopped out the car and followed Gunz's lead into the large mansion.

By the time we got to the upstairs office, I stood there in pure awe at the man that stood before me. I was completely taken back by how handsome the Haitian connect was.

He stood 6'3" with smooth dark skin dressed in a white and black striped button-up that fitted just right on his muscular build along with black dress pants and shining expensive black shoes. The diamonds off his watch, earring, and cufflinks danced under the light. I couldn't help but admire his jet black hair that was freshly cut in a low fade with a curved part on the right side. One look at him and you could tell that nigga was nothin' but a boss!

I watched as he took a puff of his Cuban cigar and looked at me with his piercing dark eyes framed by long lashes.

"Here she is boss," Gunz announced.

The connect exhaled the thick smoke from his mouth with his eyes still glued on me.

"So you are the Lady Hustla' that I've been hearing about," he said in this sexy deep voice.

"That's me," I said with a smile.

I was shocked when the connect smiled back in return, something that I wouldn't expect from a man of his stature.

"I like you Na'Tiva...you got a sense of humor. We need that sometime in our line of work. Have a seat...both of you," he directed, nodding his head over to the couch on the other side of the large office.

Without hesitation, Gunz and I walked over to the chocolate leather couch and took our seats as the connect sat across from us. I briefly glanced around and noticed a thick manila folder laid on the table placed between us. I knew it was going to be more than just getting to know each other, so I braced myself.

"I told Gunz that I wanted to meet you due to your loyalty to me and fulfilling your promise. So it was only right that I had to fulfill mine...in more ways than one," he explained.

"The reason why you are out today isn't just on your own merit. I had to use my connections that owed me favors and have them make some moves for you to get out," he informed.

"Thank you, sir," I humbly said.

"Please, call me Javel. You have proved to me your trustworthiness to call me by my name," he suggested.

I smiled. "Thank you, Javel."

"Now, onto business. As we agreed, I was to allow you into our search for B-Moore," he said, peaking my interest.

"So how's that going?" I asked.

"We found him. We have his location and we have his partner. Take a look at the folder on the table." Javel motioned to the item on the table.

"Now you may not like what you are going to see, but you need to know..." he cautioned as I grabbed the folder off the table and placed it in my lap.

Once I opened the folder, my eyes fixed on the enlarged photos of B-Moore out on the beach and in fancy restaurants. The nerve of this nigga acting like he is King mothafuckin' Tut, living the damn good life while I been through hell!

My blood boiled from anger just looking at this bitch nigga with his sick-ass smirk on his face. Yet what I saw next immediately enraged me. The next picture I came across was of none other than Na'Tya and B-Moore.

"What the fuck!" I snapped.

I flipped through the rest of the pictures only to see my sister and the man who was once my love...all cuddled up like I never existed in their world!

Chapter Three

Na'Tya

"Who would've thought we would be here together. Living off what we built," I said as I admired the beautiful landscape of the blue ocean before us.

"This is what we deserve baby. We built this empire and we are reaping the benefits," B-Moore said as he wrapped his arm around my waist and pulled me closer to him.

"Cheers to that," I said, holding up my wine glass full of champagne.

"Cheers." He nodded and clinked our glasses together.

A smile of satisfaction spread over my face. After all we been through, we finally had everything we ever wanted and more. 'Tiva was long gone, businesses were doing numbers, and I was living the high with the only man that I ever loved.

It took a long time coming for us to get to where we are now. Everything changed that spring break that Na'Tiva and B-Moore broke up while we were in high school.

Flashback:

"C'mon, girl, hurry up! I told Scooter that I was gonna be there in five," Honey nagged as I stood in front of my bathroom mirror flat ironing my hair.

"Alright, alright! I'm almost done. Damn..." I sucked my teeth and rolled my eyes in irritation. "Let me just curl my bang. You know I gotta get my swoop bang action goin'."

"Fine bitch...but then we gotta go." She sighed.

"Ok," I said as I began to curl my bang. Once my hair was finally looking fly, I slung my purse on my shoulder and made my exit out of the house.

As we walked to our destination, I realized that we were getting close to a familiar place.

"Wait a minute, I thought you said we were goin' to chill with Scooter. Why we at B-Moore's house?" I asked.

"B-Moore is having a little kickback at his crib tonight and Scooter asked if we could slide through. I mean we just coming to drink 'n' smoke, is that ok with you? Damn!" she snapped.

"Whateva'...it's just that..."

"I know. What 'Tiva did to B-Moore is fucked up, but shit, you ain't fuck that nigga ova' so he should be cool with you." Honey shrugged.

"Yeah, you right," I concurred.

"You damn right bitch. Now let's go," Honey said as she grabbed my hand and damn near dragged me up the steps of B-Moore's porch.

I let out a sigh as Honey knocked on the door. I know that we were just chillin' with B-Moore and his boys, but I didn't want no drama.

Within seconds, Honey's boo-thing Scooter opened the door. A smile quickly formed on his brown face as his eyes laid upon us.

"What up? Ya'll lookin' all good 'n' shit. C'mon in," he said before he stepped back to let us in the house.

"Ayyyyyye!" Honey yelled out as she danced to the loud music as she walked through the front door. I shook my head as I followed her into the house. That girl knew she was crazy.

As soon as we walked into the living room, my eyes immediately met with B-Moore's. He was slouched on the couch taking a hit of the large blunt. Yet I could easily see the sadness in his caramel baby face, and I knew that he was still coping with the break up from Na'Tiva.

"What up 'Tya." He nodded.

"Hey B," I said shyly, which was unlike me.

"I don't know why you ova' there acting shy 'Tya. You know you wanna come ova here and get a hit," he joked.

"Shut up B-Moore. You know I want to smoke somethin'.... Ain't nobody acting shy," I lied. "Move ova nigga," I barked as I walked over to him on the couch.

I took a seat next to him and began smoking the large blunt. As the drinks and weed filtered my system, my true feelings began to come to the surface. I laid back and watched as B-Moore bobbed his head to the Lil Wayne blasting from his stereo. I always thought he was fine, the finest nigga in Akron at that. Every girl in the city wanted to be with B-Moore, but he just had to get with my sister, 'Tiva, and look how that turned out!

B-Moore's light brown eyes snapped me out of my high trance as he caught me staring at him.

"You good?" he chuckled.

"Yeah..."

"Aiight. You over there spaced out 'n' shit. What was you thinkin' about?" he asked.

"How dumb 'Tiva was for breaking up with you," I said honestly.

His smile disappeared just hearing 'Tiva's name.

"Oh straight? Why you think that? Ain't that yo' sister?"

"Man, I don't give a fuck that she my sister. She was dead wrong for what she did to you. She supposed to hold her man down. Instead she listening to the lies her hoe ass friend was talkin' and just left you high and dry," I snapped.

"I'm just saying...she stupid for not seeing yo' full potential. She just out here gold diggin' instead of trying to build with her nigga. What type of bitch do that?" I continued speaking the real.

"That's wassup ma. That's some real shit." He nodded.

"All day...I can't be on that fake shit like 'Tiva." I shook my head. B-Moore smiled.

"I feel you. Hold that thought lil mama, I'll be right back," he said as he got up and went upstairs. I looked over to my left only to see Honey on Scooter's lap kissing on him.

"Ugh" I rolled my eyes and pulled out my phone. I scrolled through my contact list of the many niggas that would love for me to text them, but they were nowhere near the real nigga I wanted. The only one I wanted was right upstairs. I don't know if it was the liquor or the weed, but a girl was feelin' real bold, so while Honey and her boo were all caked up, I made my way upstairs.

I could see the light peak through the cracks of the closed bathroom door that was also connected to his bedroom. I shifted my way through the open door to his large room and briefly admired his decor. His family wasn't the richest, but his dad made enough money to be able to renovate the inside of their home. I felt like I was in a luxury house just at the sight of his room. I didn't have time to just stand there and look through his room, so I focused my attention on the hallway that led to the bathroom and didn't even hesitate to walk right in on him.

"Damn 'Tya...what you doing in here? If you gotta go" he began, but was cut off when I placed my index finger against his lip.

"Shh...I came in here to give you something...something you been needing," I said as I unzipped his pants.

"W-whoa...wait a minute.... What you doing?" he stammered, but I ignored him as I kneeled down, pulling his boxers and jeans down with me.

Without hesitation, I dropped down to my knees and wrapped my hands around his thick shaft. I spat on that dick and jacked him off, causing him to harden even more. He closed his eyes and tilted his head back in pleasure, and when he least expected it, I wrapped my mouth around his head and drove him to another brink of pleasure.

"Damn..." he groaned lowly as he grabbed the back of my head and pushed my mouth farther down on him. Instead of tensing up, I relaxed and deep throated him like no other. Within minutes, B-

Moore released in my mouth and I swallowed it all like a pro.

I looked up at him as I licked my lips. "Mmm..." I moaned.

"Come here," he demanded. I did as he said and got up, standing in front of him.

Grabbing me by the back of the neck, he pulled me in and kissed me. Our hands roamed each other's body, damn near tearing our clothes off.

Before I knew it, B-Moore picked me up and laid me onto his bed.

"Hold on baby.... Go slow.... This is my first time..." I whispered.

He looked at me and smiled in satisfaction. "I got you baby." He kissed me before he entered me slowly. I wrapped my legs around him as he began to take me to a new level of pain and pleasure. Once the initial pain faded, it was nothing but pure pleasure and I loved every minute of it.

From that moment, I knew that this was the first, but not the last time, me and B-Moore would do this. No matter how many times B-Moore tried to deny it, he would always end up back in the bed with me. We had to keep it a secret cause if everyone knew about me and him, it would be problems. While 'Tiva was too busy being the Reaper's girl, I was fucking the fine ass nigga she blew off.

Once 'Tiva left Akron out of the blue, everything changed. "Backstroke" by Teedra Moses blasted from my phone as I laid in my bed chillin' out. A smile formed on my face knowing that B-Moore was calling me.

"Hey baby," I gleamed.

"Wassup 'Tya. What you doin?" His sexy voice filled my ears.

"Shit, nothin'...missing you," I flirted.

"That's wassup." I could hear the smile in his voice.

"I got some shit to talk to you about. Come through," he suggested.

"Aiight. I'll see you in five."

"Aiight bet," he said before we hung up.

Slipping into my black and white striped maxi dress and my black rhinestone flip flops, I quickly pulled my hair up into a bun and made sure my lip gloss was poppin'. I had to make sure I looked good for my babe, even if this was my off day.

"I'm leavin'. I'll be back later," I yelled out to my mama who was cooped up in her room. As always, Mama was in her little depression not giving a fuck what happened to me. Just the thought about her checking out of life caused me to roll my eyes and shake my head as I closed the door behind me.

Once I arrived at B-Moore's house, we immediately went up to his bedroom.

"So what's up?" I asked as I sat on his large bed next to him.

"You know how I been tellin' you about how I need to make some more money than just workin' at my pop's place?" he led in.

"Yeah..."

"Well I got this new opportunity to make some real money with Gunz," he revealed.

"Oh foreal? Doin' what?" My eyebrow raised.

"Some street shit. Gunz's girl got a Haitian connect that can put us on so we can make that bread, and we don't have to work for Reaper and them niggas," B-Moore explained.

"Oh ok," was all I could say.

"You think I should do it?" he asked curiously. "I mean, I been doing shit the right way for so long and a nigga tired of barely makin' it. I'm eighteen fuckin' years old without a fuckin' car and ain't got shit to my name…. I'm tired of living like this." He sighed.

"I think you should take that opportunity and fuck what anybody got say about it. Do what the fuck you gotta do to make your money. I support you full fledge for that shit," I reassured.

B-Moore nodded his head in agreement. "That's why I fuck wit' you."

"Hell yeah. I'mma hold you down boo. Don't trip." I smiled before I straddled his lap and began kissing him. It had been a week since I got some of that good dick and I was ready to get my dose.

~~~

After that day, B-Moore partnered up with Gunz and started working with the new connect while I started to work for Buck. Since we were just getting our feet wet in the game, shit didn't come by easy. Our life was slowly changing as we put in the work. While B-Moore was up in the trap, I was up in the strip club with Honey doin' what the fuck I had to do to get my bread up. Some bitches would stop hustlin' all together while they man was makin' money and live off of them, but I wasn't cut like that. I learned early on from my parents that a nigga could always up and leave you. So before lettin' a nigga leave you high and dry, you betta keep workin' and save that money so you could be straight, with or without a nigga. And I'd be damned if I stopped my money flow over a nigga.

After three months of stripping at Buck's club, I had a large list of regulars who would come to the club just to see me. I was making enough money to cover Mama's bills and still have bands left over to do whatever the fuck I wanted. But I wanted more. Out of all the girls in the strip club, Big Buck always had a "Fab Five" team that was a group of his top strippers that would do private club events, traveling events, and jobs that would make them more money than the rest of us. Those bitches were gettin' paid, and I wanted to be a part it. The night I found out that one of the girls quit and moved to Houston, I was at B-Moore's house posted up.

"Damn babe...Keisha left the Fab Five!" I exclaimed as I walked back into B-Moore's bedroom after getting off the phone with Honey.

"Oh straight? You tryin' to get on?" he asked while his eyes were glued to his video game on the TV screen.

"Yeah I'm trying to get on, but I don't know." I shrugged, as I sat down on the bed.

"What you mean you don't know. Ain't you tryin' to get more money stacked up?" he asked, confused.

"Yeah...but from what I heard, bein' on the Fab Five mean you gotta do more than just dance. Some people talkin' about suckin' 'n' fuckin'," I explained.

"Hmmm..." He bit his lip while in deep thought. We sat in silence for a minute before he paused his game and turned to face me.

"Well how bad you want this money?" he asked.

"What?" I spurted out in disbelief.

"I'm sayin' 'Tya, what you want from this game? You want the money or you want the power? Do you just want to be like them other bitches and be a stripper 'til you forty 'n' shit?" he posed.

"No...I don't want to be just a stripper."

"Look, I'm not tryin' to force you to do some shit you ain't down with. I'm ya' man, so I can't have you out here gettin' fucked up...but I got a plan. We can get the money first and then take over Akron, if we follow it the right way," B-Moore brought up.

"A plan?" My face scrunched up in confusion. "What the fuck you talkin' about B?"

"Look, I heard about Buck and how he get down. That nigga got pull all ova' this fuckin' city. You get that nigga on yo' team, and with yo' fine ass and them skills you got, I know you will have that nigga sprung. If you do what you gotta do to get on the team, that'll put you in a position to get closer to Buck. And on top of that, that nigga got some powerful clients that fuck with the Fab Five. I'm talking about commissioners, mayors, even judges and shit. You get them on yo' team, shit, yo' ass can take over Buck's shit," B-Moore explained, sparking my interest.

"That's gonna help you move up in the game and take ova' Buck's shit and be a real boss ass bitch, and that's gonna help me while I run these streets. We can have the politicians and the police on our side and can't nobody stop us!" he gleamed.

"Fuck just gettin' money, 'Tya...we gonna have the money and the fuckin' power. Nobody is gonna be able to fuck with us. Me and Gunz is takin' care of Reaper so we're gonna be straight that way, and with you gettin on that Fab Five shit, we are really gonna change the game up," B-Moore continued.

I didn't have anything to say as he rambled on. All I could do was nod my head in agreement since it was a lot to take in. I never thought about shit like that, but now that he brought it up, I liked the way he was thinking.

"I'm tellin' you, 'Tya, if you just play yo' role, it will all pan out."

"Aiight, I'm with it boo," I finally said.

The next day, I was up in Buck's office tryin' to get on the Fab Five, and the rest was history.

Everything went just as B-Moore planned, all except my momma dying.

I was pained by her death, since it was so sudden and unexpected. I never thought my mother would die this soon. Even though we had our differences, she wasn't supposed to go like this.

As I sat in the dim office with Na'Tiva, sitting across the pale-faced man dressed in a black suit, I grew anxious to hear the details of my mother's insurance policy. At least I could get some of the money she earned while she was finally working and making money.

"According to your mother's life insurance policy, she listed both of you as her beneficiaries, so you will both get an equal split of the one million dollar payout. As far as the terms of Mrs. Davis's will, she designated that $150,000 from her savings will go to Na'Tiva to help cover her student loans," Mr. Corgan explained, leaving me in shock.

"Were there any other designations that she included for me?" I asked, eager to hear about what I would receive.

"Umm..." Mr. Corgan said as he scanned the document in his hand. "The only designation that she has listed for you in her will is to own her Kia Sorento," he continued.

"A Kia Sorento? What the fuck am I going to do with that?" I immediately snapped. "And there was nothing else?" I asked as I sat on the edge of my seat.

"I'm sorry, Ms. Davis"—he finally looked up at me—"but there is nothing else designated for you in her will."

"What the fuck!" I stood up full of anger. "I can't believe this bullshit! I've been there for her, even when there was no one else by her side, and this is how she does me? She gives the majority of her damn money to the daughter who damn near disowned her, and all she can give me is a funky-ass Kia Sorento? I got my own Lexus SUV and a Benz, what the fuck am I going to do with her shit?" I continued in pure anger. All I could do was shake my head as I grabbed my shit.

"I don't want to hear anything else. I'm done with this shit! Meet me out at the car when you done with this bullshit, 'Tiva," I yelled to my sister as I stormed out of the office.

My hands trembled as I dialed B-Moore's number once I approached my car.

"What the fuck," was all he could say when hearing about what just happened.

"Right! How the fuck is she gonna let 'Tiva get all her money...the same bitch who just disowned her? I'm saying like...c'mon now! Who the fuck paid her bills and made sure she was straight when her ass checked out on life?" I went off.

"It was always you.... Shit, I'm just shocked as you 'Tya. That just don't make sense.... 'Tiva don't deserve a damn thing from yo' momma," B-Moore agreed.

"Exactly! And 'Tiva is fuckin' irritating me. I knew she was gonna come up here since mama died, but she really fuckin' up our plan. I don't know if I can handle watching you and her all flirting and shit." I sighed as I sat back in my driver's seat.

"Just hold on and keep playin' yo' role. I know she fucked up the plan, but that's why we changed it

up some. Best believe she is gonna get what's comin'
to her...trust," he replied.

"I hope so cause I don't know how much I can
take," I said as I sparked up my black and mild.

"We got this baby. We're not gonna let some
scary-ass bitch ruin what we worked so hard for. I
promised you that this plan was gonna work out and
so far it has. Yeah we changed it up, but in the end
we gonna be on top while that bitch and the rest of
them niggas is gonna get what's comin' for them,"
he reassured.

"Aiight baby...I'm just gonna trust you and play
my role," I said as my eyes scanned the parking lot.
I could see Na'Tiva coming out of the building.

"Aiight, here she comes. I'll talk to you later," I
said before hanging up on him. I closed my eyes and
let out a sigh before she stepped into the car. It was

time to become actress of the year, once again. All I had to do was keep 'Tiva in Akron, and once I got what I wanted from this game, we would pin everything on her. All in due time.

Present:

The plan panned out just like B-Moore said it would, and as I stood on our patio overlooking the ocean, it panned out pretty fuckin' well. While that bitch 'Tiva was locked up because of her fuck ups, me and my man was over here living good, without a care in the world. We were finally getting what we deserved.

Chapter Four

Na'Tiva

I sat in the connect's office, still enraged by what was revealed to me about B-Moore and 'Tya.

"My men are ready to make a move whenever you're ready," Javel began. "But first, as a welcome back package, I want to make sure you are taken care of after being locked up for so long. So I'm providing you with your own place and some funds," he explained.

"Thank you."

"But"—he paused and looked at me directly in the eye–"you will be staying here in this mansion until we get B-Moore. We can't take any chances right now."

"I understand," I obliged.

"Good." He smiled. "Now how about Gunz shows you to your room so you can get nice and cleaned up for dinner tonight," Javel suggested.

"Ok," was all I could say as Gunz and I stood up and headed out of the office.

"I think he likes you," Gunz commented as we got closer to my designated room.

"That's good to hear," I replied, but I was feeling a little leery about developing this relationship with Javel.

Even a blind man could see how handsome the connect was, and a man of his stature caused bitches to flock at him, but the last thing I needed was a distraction from a nigga. I didn't know what his angle was, and if it ain't about business, I'm not with it.

"Yeah, well if you play yo' cards right with him, he'll make sure everything you want is taken care of ma. So let's see how this dinner goes," he suggested.

"Yeah, we'll see." I sighed as Gunz opened the door to my bedroom.

"Here it is," he announced. My eyes briefly scanned the large and plush luxury bedroom, impressed by the decor.

"I know how ya'll women need your alone time, so I'mma let you have it," Gunz continued.

"Aiight." I chuckled. "I'll see you later," I concluded as I stepped inside.

"Aiight bet," Gunz finished before walking away and heading downstairs.

I closed the door behind me before I approached the California king-sized bed that had a Fendi maxi dress laid out on it. I picked up the letter laid next to it and opened it up.

"Wear me," was all it said. I couldn't help but smile. Javel did have a way of charming a lady. I knew it was not the time to get caught up with a nigga, but after seeing my sister and the man who betrayed me working together, I would play the fuck out of my role to get what I wanted, and I'd do whatever I had to do to see their asses six feet under.

~~~

After taking a long-needed nap in a comfortable-ass bed, the night fell upon us and it was time to have dinner with Javel. Once I finished taking a hot shower, I slipped into the turquoise maxi dress and sandals he picked out for me and pulled my now curly hair into a high bun. It had been so long since I was in regular clothes, let alone gotten dressed up, that I barely recognized myself as I admired myself in the large bedroom mirror.

Time to fully secure my place with Javel, I thought to myself before I closed my bedroom door behind me and trailed down the spiral staircase. My eyes laid upon Javel sitting at the dining room table alone. A smile covered his face as I came to join him.

"So what are we eating?" I joked as I sat across from him.

"Something special that my cooks fixed up for us. I know it's been a long time since you had a good meal, so I made sure they gave you a wide variety,"

Javel revealed, and he wasn't lying. I watched as his two personal chefs waltzed into the dining room with rolling tables covered with plates of steak, lobster, gourmet chicken, and baked macaroni and cheese. Everything I loved! My eyes gleamed at the sight and my mouth watered. This was going to be a good-ass dinner.

I didn't hesitate to dig in and eat as soon as the plate hit the table, and I cherished every bite. Javel chuckled from the sight.

"Good huh?" he laughed.

"Yes!" I nodded as I washed down the food with my drink.

We sat in silence as we ate our meal, but it didn't take long before I completely finished my meal. Now it was time for us to have wine and get to know each other more.

"So what's your story?" he asked.

I began telling him about me and my life, no holding back. How I started off in Atlanta and one trip back to Akron because of my mother's death changed my entire life. I gave him the details of everything that had happened up until now.

"Now I'm here, sitting across from you," I said before taking my first sip of the expensive wine.

The look in his eyes told me that it was something about my unfortunate story that sparked his interest.

"We all had to go through our journey, that's what makes us stronger, and you are by far a strong woman. Life threw every wrench at you and you still aren't giving up. It's hard to find people like that Na'Tiva," Javel explained.

"Thank you," I say coyly. "What's your story?" I shot back.

He smiled in return. "Ahh, I knew you would ask me that."

"It was only right." I smiled.

"Well, I grew up very poor back in Haiti. I always had a rough life growing up," Javel began. "I watched my mother get killed right in front of me. She was at the wrong place at the wrong time when a shootout happened. Once she left, life got worse. My father struggled to put food on our table and I knew that I would never want to live like this again. I had to find a way to do better for myself, for my family." He looked me directly in the eye.

"I can understand that," I chimed in.

"So I started working for the local kingpin in my area. I was only fifteen and I did whatever I had to do to prove myself and move up in the ranks. Finally, my opportunity came and the rest was history." Javel shrugged.

"I was able to do better for me and my sister. I got us out of Haiti and worked a normal job for the first years, but resumed my business after we were official citizens. Life changed for us. The more money and power, the more problems...more threats. Soon those threats became real, and I lost the only person that meant the world to me." His eyes saddened.

"Your sister?" I said.

"Yes." Javel nodded. "A rival of mine killed her while she was at home with her newborn son. I walked in to see it...a sight that I'll never forget. My sister...my nephew." His voice quivered.

"That was many years ago." Javel sighed and looked back at me. "But that one fatal event caused me to realize what was truly important in my life. I worked so hard to do better for my family, and in the end, because of this lifestyle, I lost them. I want to have a family, you know? I want to be able to build that unit of love and support and do things right.... It's just hard to find that one. Hard to find someone loyal and understanding to this life," he continued.

"I agree." I took a sip of my drink.

"I think that after you claim your revenge, it will cause you to regain focus of your life and what direction you want to go in. I think we get so caught up in this life and getting back at those who have done us wrong, we lose ourselves. Then after we successfully get that revenge, we are back to square one," Javel said, shedding his wisdom.

"I feel like I'm already at square one. Can't get no worse than coming out of jail," I confessed.

"True. I've been there, in more ways than one 'Tiva. I may look young, but I've had experience in my forty years of life." He grinned, leaving me in disbelief.

"Forty!" I exclaimed. "You don't look a day over twenty-seven. Yo' ass gotta be lyin'." I gave him the side eye. Javel chuckled in response.

"Nope. One thing that I don't do is lie."

"That's why I like you. You seem like a straight shoota'." My liquor started talking.

"Same here. You remind me of the female version of myself Na'Tiva. That is why I allowed you to stay in my home. Not too many can stay here, but you showed me that you are unlike the others." He paused.

"So, we will take a couple of weeks to get you settled and prepared for taking out B-Moore. Then when you are ready, we will make a move. We don't want to wait too long before he and his accomplice leave," Javel suggested.

"Good. Cheers to making those mothafuckas pay!" I said, raising my glass.

"Cheers," he said before clinking our glasses together.

~~~

After my dinner with Javel, I spent my days planning what I wanted to do when I got B-Moore and Na'Tya in my presence. I've been thinking about this day for so long while I was in prison, and

I wanted to make sure that everything goes smoothly when I finally got the opportunity.

I sat in my bed mapping out my plan onto the pages of my notepad. I was so deeply engrossed in writing my plan that I barely heard my new phone ringing.

"Hello." I spoke into the phone.

"What up?" The voice of Gunz filled my ear.

"Nothin', just planning for what's about to go down."

"I see you. You always stay ten steps ahead of them, that's wassup," he said. I couldn't help but smile at his compliment.

"You already know. So what's goin' on?" I asked as I laid back onto my bed.

"I got some shit to handle as far as work, wanted to see if you wanted to roll with me," Gunz suggested.

"Aiight, I'm down."

"Good. I'll see you in twenty."

"Aiight see you then," I said before hanging up our call.

Just as Gunz said, he arrived within twenty minutes parked in front of Javel's estate. I hopped into his truck and was immediately greeted by Gunz holding three thick-ass envelopes.

"Here," he said as he handed them to me.

"What's this?" I asked with a raised eyebrow.

"That's yo' cut." He nodded.

"My cut?" I said, puzzled.

"Yeah. That's yo' cut from our earnings while you was gone," he informed.

I rushed to open one of the envelopes to see nothing but bands of hundreds. I counted the money in one envelope to find that there was $50,000 in just one.

"You foreal?" I asked, astonished.

"Hell yeah ma. I couldn't just leave you hangin' while you was locked up. I had to make sure you straight when you came back," he answered as he started the car back up and began to drive out the driveway.

"Damn...I don't even know what to say.... Thank you," I said, damn near speechless.

"Always ma. You know I got you. Shit, you saved a nigga's life. That's the least I can do."

"You didn't have to do that Gunz," I disclosed.

"But I wanted to," he interjected, looking me dead in the eye.

"I know." I looked down. "Thanks Gunz," I said gratefully.

He looked back to the road and smiled. "Now yo' ass can go shopping and do that girly shit you like," he joked.

"Shut up!" I laughed, playfully smacking him on the arm.

"You know my ass is not going shopping. Shit if anything, I'mma invest this money," I continued.

"That's what a smart woman do," he coined in.

"Hell yeah. Especially after I take care of them fuckers, I want to have some clean money coming in," I said as I sat back in my seat.

"That's the plan... I don't know if I can do that though." He shrugged.

"Why you say that?" I asked curiously.

"I don't see myself getting out of this game that easy ma. Yeah you can get out cause you a woman. You can get married to a real nigga that's making money and you can live the lavish life that you're used to living. But that's not my case. I have to be able to provide for me and my family. I'm not a business type of nigga like B-Moore or Javel. I'm gritty...I get shit done and do what needs to be done. I don't mind gettin' down and dirty, killin' niggas or whateva'. I can't be no suit 'n' tie nigga," he explained.

"Damn," was all I could say.

"Yeah, not something you used to hearin' huh? Niggas be lying talking about how they are gonna get out and be clean. Ain't shit out here for me. This is all I know now. I'mma live by the gun and die by the gun. But I don't want to leave this earth without leaving my legacy. A child, you know?" he continued, shedding light about himself.

"Yeah, I feel you," I commented as we pulled up in the back parking lot of a warehouse.

"Aiight, I don't want you to get caught up in this shit. You just came out the pen and you don't need no heat right now. I just wanted you to ride with me. So just stay put for a minute while I handle this business with the crew," he said.

"Ok," I agreed, and watched as he hopped out the car and headed into the warehouse. It didn't take long before he reappeared from the building.

"Everything good?" I asked.

"Yep. Everything is all good. I got a few more stops and then after that we can head back to my crib and have a drink. I know yo' ass need one," he replied.

"Hell yeah!" I exclaimed, causing him to chuckle.

"Aiight bet," he said as he drove off to the next location.

~~~

"So this is how you living now?" I asked as we walked into his large mansion.

"You already know, business has been hella good." He smiled as we walked into his black and white living room.

"That's what I like to hear. Even when a girl was locked up, you was still holding it down," I said as I sat on his black leather L couch.

"Hell yeah. I'm always about my business. I wasn't about to have you come outta jail flat out broke. I made sure to break off your cut while you was gone," Gunz explained before he headed into the kitchen to get our drinks.

"That's why I respect you Gunz," I announced as I sat back and relaxed, something that I hadn't done in a long time.

"Thanks ma," Gunz replied as he walked back with two glasses of Hennessy and Coke in both hands.

He sat next to me and cut on his stereo with his remote control. J. Cole's new album began playing through his surround sound.

"That's yo' shit huh?" I joked.

"Hell yeah. He be speakin' real shit. I fuck with him," Gunz replied.

"Ok, I feel you," I said before taking a sip of my drink.

We continued talking and kept the drinks flowing. We both felt relaxed and in our comfort zone, enjoying each other's company. Before I knew it, Gunz laid his head on my lap and revealed some things about him I never knew, but there was one thing that was eating at me and I was dying to know.

"Javel told me about his sister and her baby getting murdered. Was that-" I began, but was cut off.

"Yes. That was my son," Gunz said, sitting up and looking away. I could tell this was a touchy topic for him and almost regretted the fact that I brought it up.

"I'm sorry," I said softly.

"It's aiight ma. I know you want to know more about it. I came to grips with this shit. Took me years to be able to even talk about it," he shared.

"Who did it?" I asked.

"A fuck nigga named Damon. He was one of Javel's competition and wanted to hit Javel where it would hurt," he sneered.

"I didn't want to leave her that night." His face softened. "But I had to handle this work, and I told her that I was gonna come right back. Shit took longer than I thought. And when I came back..." His voice trailed off as his jaw locked.

"When I came back, blood was everywhere and the shit that I saw I can never get rid of," Gunz revealed. I could not only see the pain in his eyes, but I could feel it. The mere thought of losing someone you love and your child on top of that would make a person want to cry, but to experience it was a whole other level of pain and suffering. Just seeing him relive this made me want to cry.

"What happened to the nigga who did it?" I had to know.

"Me and Javel found that fuck nigga, set his ass up real good. Once we had his ass in our possession, we cut that niggas balls off and skinned his ass alive.

Then we let that mothafucka burn. We sat there and watched his ass die and it still wasn't enough justice. But it was enough to make me feel better that we made his ass pay. I wanted him to suffer just like Chantale and Corey did," Gunz explained.

"I feel you," I said, nodding my head in agreement.

"Yeah..." He sighed. "That's why I feel for you. You been through so much since you got back to Akron and I understand how it feels to want to kill those who fucked you over in the worse way. I know 'Tya is your sister 'n' all, but what she did to you was some unforgivable shit. It's like, damn, did she have that shit planned all along? Did her and B-Moore map that shit out, ready to bring you down?" he posed, sparking my interest.

My thoughts ran wildly. Maybe they did have that shit planned out and I was just a pawn in their game. My blood boiled at the thought.

"They had to have had this shit planned. It's just fucked up that they would do some fucked up shit behind my back. I almost died while I was in lockup. You remember when you found out about that," I said.

"Yeah, I remember. I came to see you after you recovered. If they let me come see you while you was in the hospital I would've," Gunz said sincerely.

"I know." I looked up at him. Gunz was already handsome, but it was his heart and his care for me that pulled me into him more. Ever since life had brought us together, he's became a pivotal partner in my life. Something that I never had. Not with B-Moore and not with Reaper.

"I worked hard to find them for you 'Tiva. I know how it feels when you want to get justice but don't know where to start. Me and Javel worked hard, but we got them niggas. But there is one thing you gotta do before you kill them," he suggested.

"What?" I asked in confusion.

"I'm just saying, since you want to get rid of B-Moore and 'Tya, you need to be skilled at this. Saying you want to kill someone is one thing, but doing it is another," Gunz replied.

"Right," I agreed.

"I want to make sure yo' ass is a pro before you get down there and fuck it up cause 'Tya is pulling on yo' heartstrings and you let emotions get the best of you cause that's your sister. Or you get down there and can't even shoot," Gunz reasoned.

"So we need to do some work on that before you make your move aiight?" he continued.

"Ok. I'm down with that." I paused and looked at him.

"Why are you doing all this for me Gunz? I know you said you can relate and want to help, but even before this, you been here by my side, looking out for me. I mean, you don't have to do all of that. So why do all this for me?" I interrogated.

Gunz looked away for a minute and gazed at the burning wood in the fireplace, as if he was in deep thought before looking back at me with sincere eyes.

"You saved a nigga's life. I know you take it lightly when I say it, but when you are on the brink of death and someone almost sacrifices themselves to help you escape meeting yo' maker, you gain a sense of appreciation for not only them but for life. I don't have many people left in my life that proved their loyalty to me like you, and I want to hold on to that. Whateva I can do to help make ya' life better, I'll do that, cause I know you would do the same for me, ma'. I ain't about to get all emotional 'n' shit, but a nigga got mad love for you 'Tiva, and I want to not just say that but show you that," Gunz revealed.

I don't know if it was the liquor or the fact that I really had feelings for Gunz that I always pushed under the surface, but without a second thought, I leaned in and planted a kiss onto his full and soft lips. Shocked by what I just did, I pulled away and looked at him. Gunz peered at me with his round brown eyes and licked his luscious lips before grabbing the back of my neck and kissing me passionately. I closed my eyes and enjoyed the pleasure I was feeling just from one kiss as Gunz laid me down on his couch. He hands roamed my body as we both undressed each other. I immediately got wet just from one look at his tattooed, muscular body. I bit my bottom lip as my hands trailed down his six pack and defined V-cut. *Damn! I wanted him.*

I pulled down his boxers and what I saw put me in pure delight. His thick nine inches stood at attention, ready for me to get a taste. I licked my lips before wrapping my mouth around it and sending him to pure ecstasy from my head game.

"Fuck 'Tiva!" He groaned as he grabbed a handful of my hair and pushed me farther onto his shaft, causing me to deep throat him. Before he could release, he pushed me off him and back onto the couch.

Wrapping my legs around his shoulders, he shoved his dick inside me, causing me to gasp in excitement. His thickness felt so good inside my warmth. It's been so long since I had some, and to feel Gunz inside me caused me to get even wetter.

My legs shook as he pumped in and out of me, hitting my g-spot each and every time. My nails dug into the skin on his arms as I held for dear life as he beat my pussy up. Tears of pleasure flowed from my eyes as I began orgasming right then and there.

Before I could take a breather, he turned me over and began hitting it from the back. I gripped onto the armrest as he pounded me into submission. Everything about this was intense, and I loved every moment of it. I needed this. I wanted this. As we came in unison, I knew that this was not going to be the last time we did this.

The next week, Gunz and I went to go handle some business and get my practice in.

"This nigga been owing us money for a while, so he needs to get taken care of," Gunz announced as we pulled up to the location.

"Aiight, I'm down," I replied before we hopped out of the car and entered the black night.

My six-inch heels clicked against the cement ground as we walked into the dark alley. As soon as we went deeper into the darkness, my eyes met with the three figures standing underneath a light post near the trash bins. Two were standing upright while one was positioned on their knees.

Once we got closer I could see the man's round and brown face clearly. Fear crept over his face when his eyes connected with Gunz's.

"I-I'm sorry..." he sputtered.

"Nigga, yo' ass will be sorry by the time I get done with you," Gunz said coldly as he hovered above the man.

"Please...we can work this out," the man pleaded.

"Work this out?" Gunz laughed. "Nigga yo' ass been avoiding me like the fuckin' plague. You know you been owing us money for months now, and since you can't pay up with dollas...you know what's about to happen," he continued.

"No...no...I can pay you the money. I can pay you," the man reasoned, but it fell upon deaf ears as Gunz looked over to me, giving me the okay to take this nigga out.

As the man continued to beg and plead, I pulled out the gun that was tucked in the back of my jeans and gripped the gun with my gloved hand. I looked at the man with not an ounce of pity as he turned his attention to me and begged me not to do it. I simply visualize his face as B-Moore's and let the bullet silence him once and for all. I looked at the man's dead body and felt a rush of adrenaline.

"Aiight, take care of this shit," Gunz said to the two men. "C'mon 'Tiva, let's roll," he commanded.

Not another word was said as we walked back to the car. For such a horrendous act, I actually felt liberated. Like I was a bitch that was not to be fucked with.

"I did it!" I surged with excitement.

"I know. You didn't even shake or hesitate. I'm proud of you ma'," he complimented as we drove off.

"But you need more practice," Gunz said seriously. "Just cause this goes good don't mean it will go good the next time. You gotta be prepared for these things. And I'mma make sure you ready," he stressed, and just like he said we practiced numerous times.

Every time he had to take a nigga out, he called me to come with him and finish them off. Whenever I made the final kill, I would see B-Moore or 'Tya's face to help me do what needed to be done. I began enjoying this a little too much, but I couldn't wait til I got to do that to the two mothafuckas that betrayed me.

Within those few weeks and planning and training, I not only got closer with Gunz but I got closer to Javel. Just as planned, I entertained the connect with everything but my body. I gave him the queen companionship that I knew he'd been searching for. Private dinners at night, intimate conversations, and being a listening ear to him. I could tell he'd been lonely and all he needed was a companion, so I played my role. Since I established my place with him, I had a wide variety of things to help me get my revenge. Now it was time to take a trip to Miami!

Chapter Five

Na'Tiva

I peered out of the window and took in the view of Florida as I sat on Javel's private jet. I took a sip of my Chardonnay as Gunz and the henchmen sat behind me talking about the new Future mixtape that just dropped while Javel furiously typed away at an email about his legit businesses. I let out a sigh and sat back in my seat. This was the calm before the storm, but I surely was ready for this.

Excitement surged through my body as we finally landed in Miami. Time to make shit happen! I hopped off the jet and took in the cool breeze and warm sun that greeted me as our henchmen grabbed our bags.

"Let's go...we got moves to make," Javel commanded as he wrapped his arm around my waist and began to lead me toward our limousine that was parked nearby. I looked over to my right to see Gunz's eyes glued on me, and I instantly felt a pang of guilt. I'd been fuckin' with Gunz on the low ever since our first encounter, but here I was playing my role with Javel. I looked away and focused my attention onto the driver holding the car door open for us.

"Thank you," I said politely before sliding into the limo with Javel. I watched as Gunz and the other henchmen slipped into the other limo before we pulled off.

"Your time is coming.... How you feelin?" Javel asked as we were on route to one of his estates.

"Ready to take them bitches out," was all I could say in response.

He smiled. "Don't forget what I said "Tiva. Think about what you want out of life after this," he suggested.

"I will," I said before looking out the window. I was in no mood to talk, just ready to take action.

Once we got to Javel's house, we got settled in and began putting our plan in motion. I had to play it low key to find out my sister and B-Moore's daily routine. After a week of establishing their routine, I thought about going under cover to ambush them but decided against it. There was no need to go about it in hiding. I wanted them to see my face and know I was here.

"You sure about this ma?" Gunz asked me as we pulled up to the local nightclub that B-Moore and 'Tya steadily frequented.

"Yes. Very sure," I gleamed before hopping out the car and making my way to the entrance of the club. All eyes were on me as I walked into the club with my crew of men behind me. I was dressed to impress in my red Antonio Berardi dress and six-inch heels, like I never left the game.

I sauntered my way up the stairs to the V.I.P. section, and to see the mixture of surprise and anger that was spread across my sister's face made me smile with pleasure!

"Why so serious? Ya'll wasn't expecting me to join the party?" I joked as I stood in front of the couple sitting on the couch.

I grabbed the bottle of champagne out of their booth, popped it open, sending the cork flying in their direction, and began to take a swig of it.

"Hmm, I see your taste in champagne is still cheap. Can't expect much from a ratchet bitch like yourself," I directed to Na'Tya. "And I see you still using your old tricks to woo the women huh? I remember when you did this for me. Thought you would've changed it up for yo' other bitch." I looked over at B-Moore.

B-Moore's jaw locked in anger.

"Bitch, you got some mothafuckin' nerves!" 'Tya spat as she hopped out of her seat in an attempt to charge at me, but was suddenly stopped by one of the nigga's that was rolling with me.

I tisked loudly while moving my finger. "Uh, Uh, Uhh, I wouldn't do that if I were you," I cautioned.

"What the fuck you want 'Tiva?" Na'Tya spat.

"I just came to show my face, and let you know that the best woman is back in the game. So if I was ya'll, I would watch my back.... You never know what could happen when you turn your head and ignore the signs," I taunted with a smile.

Before 'Tya and B-Moore could retaliate, my crew of men blocked them as I left the V.I.P. section and got lost in the crowd. Before they could even leave their section, I would already be gone out the club.

Chapter Six

Na'Tya

My blood boiled from what just happened. How the fuck did she get out and how did this bitch find out that me and B-Moore was in Miami? So many thoughts flooded through my mind as me and B-Moore stormed out the V.I.P. section and rushed down the stairs.

"What the fuck was all that about 'Tya?" B-Moore yelled as we walked out the club.

"I don't fuckin' know!" I snapped.

"How the fuck could they know where we at, and how the fuck did she get out?" he said angrily, as if it was my fault. I immediately got in defense.

"The fuck if I know!" I shot back.

"We gotta get the fuck outta here," B-Moore said, looking around.

Before I could say anything, he grabbed my arm and damn near dragged me toward the parking lot where our car was parked.

Once B-Moore unlocked the car with the car remote, our 2015 Mercedes Benz C-Class blew up into bits. We ducked down as the flames engulfed the air. When we finally stood up and looked at the burning automobile, I was filled with anger.

If this bitch wants to go to war, then I'mma bring her ass Armageddon!

Na'Tiva

Three days passed after my incident with 'Tya and B-Moore at the club. That night had set our plan in motion. Gunz was keeping tabs on the two as I continued to make sure we had everything set up. Placing my black leather jacket over my plain white tee, I pulled my hair back into a ponytail and decided to go out and get something to eat. I couldn't be cooped up in this mansion for too long.

I walked towards the front door and opened it, only to see one of my hitmen standing there with a serious facial expression. I stepped out of the doorway and stood on the porch with him.

"What's up?" I questioned while folding my arms.

"The boss has a new location for Tya and B-Moore. The rest of the crew is already on the move there, so we got to leave now!" he urged.

I stood there for a moment, confused for a minute before following the hitman to the vehicle he had waiting for us. After climbing into the passenger seat of the car, we quickly pulled off from Javel's estate. The man and I drove down the service drive in silence, but I couldn't shake this feeling that something was off. If the plans had changed, why didn't Javel or Gunz hit me up?

I looked over at the hitman who was driving the car suspiciously. I searched through my memory trying to remember where I had seen him before when it finally hit me! He was there that night at the club when I confronted 'Tya and B-Moore, but the only thing was he wasn't with me, he was on 'Tya and B-Moore's side! I quickly focused my attention back out the window, trying to figure out my next move.

With the fast-paced speed that the car was going at, I couldn't hop out of the car. *But at this point, that might be my best option right now.* Just as that thought crossed my mind, I saw out of the reflection of my window the man pulling out a gun. Turning around quickly, I grabbed ahold of his hand and struggled to get the gun out of his hand. The car swerved all over the road as I tried to pry his fingers loose.

Two rounds went off in the car with one grazing my forehead. Ignoring the stinging pain, I finally was able to get the gun out of his hand. But what happened next was unexpected!

A loud blaring sound of a semi-truck horn grabbed my attention. A couple of inches in front of us was a semi-truck flying toward us. Without even thinking I grabbed the wheel, jerking it to the right, sending the car flying off the road and crashing into a tree, causing me to hit my head on the dashboard. Feeling my head spinning due to the impact, I weakly tried to exit the car. Fumbling around, I tried to unbuckle my seat belt as I felt my vision starting to get blurry.

"Not now! I have to get out this car!" I yelled, infuriated by the fact that I felt a blackout coming on. *I can't die...not like this,* was my last thought before I blacked out.

Chapter Seven

Na'Tiva

Pained throbbed from the back of my head as I slowly opened my eyes. I looked around only to find myself in an unfamiliar room. I tried to move, but my attempt failed when I realized that I was strapped up to a chair.

"You thought you got away huh bitch?" The familiar voice came from behind me. When the person walked in front of me, my eyes met with Na'Tya's as she stood over me with brass knuckles on one hand and a gun in the other.

I scrunched my face up in pure disgust at the mere sight of her and hacked up a glob of spit at her. "Fuck you bitch. You thought you got away but I found yo' rat ass with that fuck nigga," I said, but was met with a hard punch in my fuckin' mouth, causing my head to fly back.

"Shut the fuck up!" she yelled as she continuously punched me with her brass knuckles like a punching bag.

"I'm tired of yo' ass always talking. That's all yo' bitch ass is good for 'Tiva. But I'm not like yo' prissy ass. I'm the bitch that will take yo' ass out. Don't you ever forget that!" she roared.

Each blow to my face and body stung as my vision slowly began to blur once again and blood poured from my nose, temple, and mouth. All I could do was sit there and take it as 'Tya continued to wail out on me. I flowed in and out of consciousness as she began to talk.

"You thought you had this shit on lock huh 'Tiva?" She laughed.

"You really thought I was fuckin' with you and we were on good terms...after all the shit you did to me? After you left me and Mama high and dry to fend for our fuckin' selves? You was living the high fuckin' life with Reaper, getting money but didn't even think twice to break bread with yo' own fuckin' family that was strugglin'? Who the fuck does that 'Tiva?" she ranted.

"You treated that bitch Danielle better than you treated yo' own fuckin' sister. You was gettin' paid and didn't even think twice about if me and Mama had food to eat. Yo' ass was so stuck on stupid for that nigga that you didn't even think about me and Mama barely surviving. Especially when you left. Talkin' about we family my ass bitch! You ain't nothing but another bitch in the streets. My sister died a long time ago when she turned her back on me and mines. As far as I'm concerned, I don't know who the fuck this bitch is sitting in front me," she continued, revealing her real emotions towards me.

B-Moore laughed as he came out from the shadows. He was in here this whole time!

He grabbed me by my hair and pulled my head up.

"Bitch you know you fucked up right? Showin' yo' fuckin face like you the top-notch bitch. Blowing up my car like you on some boss shit. I'mma burn yo' ass alive and watch you die tonight like I should have done a long time ago," he spat. My body filled with anger, but I was too weak to do anything.

A man busted into the room clearly out of breath, causing 'Tya and B-Moore to look at him in annoyance.

"What's the problem?" B-Moore asked, releasing my hair from his grip.

"Yeah, don't you see we in the middle of something!" Tya spat in anger.

"The connect is here! Him and a bunch of his goons stormed into the place. It's just a matter of seconds before they get here," he concluded.

Struggling, I lifted my head and saw that 'Tya and B-Moore's faces were filled with turmoil at the news. They looked at each other before heading toward the exit. But 'Tya stopped in her tracks.

"Finish her off," she commanded, before she finally left the room. The man nodded his head and pulled out his gun and walked towards me. Anger welled in my body once again.

"Get back here you fucking coward! You running around here like you some boss bitch and you can't even finish a job! Fuck you 'Tya!" I yelled out before the man pistol whipped me, causing me to spit out blood. My jaw was throbbing in pain as I slowly turned my head back to look at the man who now had his gun aimed at my head. I closed my eyes in defeat. After all this I was going to die like a fucking dog strapped to a chair with no means to defend myself. *Fuck it!* I opened my eyes only to see the man with a sick grin on his face.

Just then Javel busted into the room and shot the man at point blank range in the head. Blood splattered all over me as the man's body dropped to the ground, twitching violently. Rushing quickly to my side, Javel cupped my face. "Are you ok?" he asked sincerely.

"Yeah..." I choked out before my eyes flooded with tears. I couldn't hold back my feelings any longer. I cried like a newborn baby.

"It's ok, I got you," he said reassuringly before untying me and hoisting me into his arms like a princess. Javel carried me out of the building, which was now filled with mounds of the bodies of 'Tya and B-Moore's henchmen. I rested my head against Javel's chest and cried softly.

Chapter Eight

"You're gonna be ok," Javel reassured me as we sat in the back seat of the car.

"I'm going to take you to one of my hospitals and they are going to take good care of you. I promise." He held me tightly as the driver sped down the highway.

Before I knew it, I fell asleep in his arms. Once I woke up, I found myself in a large hospital room with Javel by my side.

"How you feeling?" he asked as he sat up.

"I don't know...still feel like I've been hit by a truck." I let out a slight chuckle. "How long have I been out?" I asked as I looked around the spacious room that was styled as if it were a five-star hotel suite.

"A few days. You were in critical condition, almost had a concussion," Javel explained.

"Damn," I said as I struggled to reach for the cup of water planted on the table in front of me.

"Here, let me help you," Javel insisted as he grabbed the pink cup and moved it closer for me to use.

"Thanks," I simply said as I began to take my drink.

I wasn't used to a man taking care of me while I was in the hospital. The last person who provided care for me while I was in the hospital was my sister. Now here I was, because of that bitch who caught me slippin'.

"Where is Gunz and the men?" I interrogated. I was surprised that Gunz wasn't here.

"He is heading up the team and looking for 'Tya and B-Moore. We can't let them escape that easy," Javel informed.

"Right." I nodded my head. Just the thought of them raised my blood pressure, so I decided to change the subject.

"What hospital are we at? This is a fancy-ass room for just one patient," I chimed in.

"This is one of my privately owned hospitals. I have a few of them spread out in different states," he shared.

"Oh yeah?" I looked at him in disbelief.

"Yes. I always wanted to diversify my money. Health care is a good investment...Maybe after this, I could put you on." Javel smiled.

"I'd like that," I mused.

"Good. But you need to rest," he suggested "I'm not going to leave you. I'll be right here when you wake up."

"Ok," I said as I laid back and watched the latest reality show playing on the flat screen TV. If only my life were as simple as some of these housewives' lives. That should have been me if I never went back to Akron. I would still be with Damien...married to him at that, and living the high life as an athlete's wife. Instead, I got dragged into the life of the streets and became a cold-blooded killer that got betrayed by the people that I once loved.

I rolled over facing the wall and let a single tear stroll down my face, pained by the thought of how my life had drastically changed. One decision. One event. One bad move and here I was playing this sick game of life and death. But I'd be damned if I died before seeing 'Tya and B-Moore get what they deserved. A new sense of determination flowed through my veins before I finally fell asleep.

Once I was finally discharged from the hospital, Javel took me to his secluded high-rise condo and tended to my every want and need. He was so caring and attentive to me that I almost forgot about what was going on outside in the real world. It was just me and this sexy-ass chocolate man that catered to me.

"Mmm..." I moaned as I laid back onto the couch and tilted my head back from the pleasure I was receiving from Javel giving me a foot massage.

"Feels good huh?" His deep voice filled my ears.

"Yes..." I said softly.

"I knew you needed it. You been so tense. I'm going to have Miriam come and give you a full body. Unless..." He paused as his hands moved up my leg, working out the kinks.

"Unless what?" I pushed further.

"Unless you want me to give you one." The way he said it made my pussy throb. Who wouldn't want a fine-ass man like him to put his hands on her? I bit my lip, trying to pull myself out of my naughty thoughts.

"Hmm, is your full body gonna feel like this?" I hinted.

"It'll feel better. I guarantee that." He licked his full lips.

"Mmm, well I'd rather have you do that over Miriam," I teased.

Javel flashed me his Colgate smile, causing me to instantly get wet.

"How about you go to the room, get undressed, and put on that robe in the bathroom. I'll meet you up there in five minutes," he instructed.

"Ok," I replied before getting up and heading upstairs to the master bedroom. I'd never do something like this, but shit...I'd been wanting a piece of Javel from the very first day I laid my eyes on him. From his smooth skin, large muscles, and sexy facial features...I wanted him, and acting like a companion to him wasn't hard to do. Hiding my sexual attraction to him was another thing.

I went upstairs and did as he said. I slipped out of my sundress, leaving me only in a thong, and slid on the plush white robe. I laid onto the California king-sized bed and relaxed as I waited on him. To make it easier for him, I slid down the robe to just cover my ass, exposing my bare back as I laid on my stomach.

My eyes quickly opened when I felt his arm and oiled hands soothingly rub on my lower back. His hands glided all over my back and neck, slowly working out the kinks that I had from pent-up frustration. I bit my bottom lip as his hands finally palmed my round ass cheeks and began massaging them. I wanted him so bad, and Javel could sense it. In one swift motion he slid my thong down, causing me to arch my back. My body went into a shock when his mouth connected with my pussy and he began to eat me from the back.

"Ohhh fuck!" I moaned out as his tongue worked feverishly against my clit. I gripped the pillows as my legs trembled in pleasure. I couldn't take it anymore as I came in his mouth.

"Mmm, turn that ass around," he commanded as he sat up in the bed. Without hesitation, I did what I was told. I laid on my back and admired his sexy, naked body. Tattoos adorned his muscular body, from his chest to his arms to his back. Damn!

My eyes trailed down his eight pack to his thick and long ten inches. He leaned down and kissed me passionately as his hands roamed my thick curves. My eyes closed and a slight moan escaped my lips as he kissed and licked on the hot spot on my neck.

"I want to see your sexy ass while you take this dick," he whispered in my ear before sitting back on his knees in the bed.

Holding my legs up, Javel slid his hardened member inside my wet and throbbing pussy, instantly connecting with my g-spot. It was as if my pussy was made for him, and as he began stroking me slowly, I knew I was in a world of trouble.

My whole body quivered as he picked up his speed, causing me to squirt all over his dick numerous times. Out of all my years, my body never reacted like this, and I loved every minute of it. With my legs still wrapped around his waist, he held my ass firmly in his hands as I wrapped my arms around his neck, holding on for dear life as he stood up in the middle of the room. I tilted my head back in pure ecstasy as he pumped ravishly inside my pussy while standing up.

"Fuck Javel! Damnnnnn," I screamed out as he pounded me to another orgasm.

"Come all over this dick!" he said in his sexy voice, causing my pussy to quiver as I came hard.

Laying me back onto the bed, Javel continued working in and out of me until he came inside of me.

"Damn..." he said as we both laid in the bed catching our breath. Not another word was said as we laid there in each other's arms and fell instantly asleep.

When we both woke up hours later, we took a shower together and embarked on another round in the bathroom, and a third round back in the bedroom. Each and every time it got better and better, making me fall in love with the brilliant man known as the connect.

~~~

The next morning I woke up to the smell of freshly cooked pancakes and bacon. Slipping the robe over my naked body, I headed downstairs only to see Javel cooking in the kitchen in nothing by his black cotton pajama pants and his bare, muscular upper body exposed.

"You cook too?" I smiled as I sat at the kitchen island.

"Being single for so long, a man has to know how to cook," he said as he fixed my plate and sat it in front of me.

"That's good to know," I said as I began to dig my fork into my eggs. "Thanks for this Javel," I continued before eating.

"No, thank you 'Tiva.... We both needed that last night," he replied as he sat next to me with his plate.

As we were eating and flirting, Javel's phone rung, interrupting our moment of bliss.

"Hold on," he said to me as his face became serious at the name on the caller id.

"Hello." He spoke into the phone.

"Yeah...so what happened?...Did you find them?...Only one huh?...Aiight...Let's make it happen...Aiight, thanks," he said before hanging up the phone and snapping me back into our harsh reality.

"That was Gunz," Javel announced. Just the mentioning of his name caused the guilt of me fucking Javel to slowly creep up on me.

"Oh yeah? What's going on?" I asked, pushing my emotions to the side and focusing on business.

"They got the location on them...but the problem is, we only have 'Tya. B-Moore is missing. Can't trace a location on him right now. So what you want to do?" Javel questioned.

"We'll find B-Moore, but for now let's take care of that bitch," I said, fully determined about what was about to go down.

"Aiight. I'll call them and tell them that we are about make a move," Javel said, grabbing his phone and leaving me alone in the kitchen.

A smile of satisfaction covered my face. It was time to make moves.

Chapter Nine

Na'Tya

"You have reached the voice mail..." the automated message greeted me on the other end of the phone before I threw it against the wall. *Where the fuck was he at?* I asked myself as I walked toward the living room and plopped down on the couch. B-Moore had been M.I.A. for a week now, and each and every time I called him it went straight to voice mail. Picking up my glass of Hennessy, I took a big swig and placed it back down on the coffee table. Ever since that day 'Tiva was rescued from the hideout, B-Moore had been acting real funny. He kinda acted like he was scared of something, and every time I would ask him about it, he would blow it off like it was nothing.

I should have realized something was up with him because two days later I woke up and he was gone! It's been a week now and there was no sign of him nowhere. Now rolling a blunt alone in our second estate, I grabbed the remote and turned on my CD player and blasted Khia's "Don't Trust No Nigga."

Feeling the drink course through my system, I stood up, letting my silk robe fly open and expose my black lingerie nightie. Licking the blunt, I grabbed the lighter to seal it as I bobbed my head to the music. Sparking the blunt, I inhaled the high-grained weed into my lungs. Plopping back onto the couch, I rapped along with Khia while continuing my personal pity party.

After everything I did for B-Moore, this was how he repaid me? Betrayed wasn't even the word to describe how I felt right now. I sacrificed everything for that nigga! Grabbing the remote once again, I turned on the TV and switched it to the surveillance mode. Checking around the outside of the crib, I suddenly saw a group of people on the side of the house. Zooming in, I saw 'Tiva with a bunch of niggas making their way to the side entrance of my crib. I let out a little laugh before taking another swig of my drink. *So this is how it's going to end huh? Fuck it! If this is how it's going to end then so be it. I'm tired of this shit.*

The thought filled my mind as I downed the rest of my drink and took another long drag of my blunt. By the time 'Tiva and her goon of niggas traveled through my home, I was finishing the blunt. Putting the blunt out, I stood up and faced my sister, who stood there with her gun aimed at me.

"So what you 'bout to do then bitch?" I asked 'Tiva, challenging her gangsta. A surprise expression filled 'Tiva's face before she barked orders to her goons to tie me up. Holding out my wrists, I willingly allowed them to tie them while all

I could do was smile. Seeing my sister act so tough was just so amusing.

'Tiva's goons followed her lead out toward the beach where they boarded me on a boat and set sail. 'Tiva glared at me while the boat bumped against the waves. I chuckled again while looking back toward the home that B-Moore and I once shared. We were so far off at sea I could barely make out my home from the other beach homes. One of the goons slowed down the boat and killed the engine. I focused my attention back on 'Tiva, who was now hovering over me as she held her gun tightly in her hand.

"What's on yo' mind 'Tiva? I know you ain't bring me out here for nothing, so if you going to kill me go ahead and get it over with instead of wasting fucking time," I spat. Full of frustration, 'Tiva beat me mercilessly over and over again with the butt of her gun. The whole left side of my face throbbed as I spit blood out of my mouth.

"Where the fuck is B-Moore?" she questioned, which made me laugh.

"How the hell should I know?" I sassed.

"You think this is a fucking joke huh?" she asked while turning around. "Throw that hoe into the water," she commanded.

"Oh, so you going to drown me hoe? You a weak-ass bitch! You can't even get your hands dirty like a real nigga. Instead you just taking the easy way out," I challenged.

'Tiva looked over at me and didn't say a word as her goons threw me overboard. Greeted by the cold water, I started to kick my legs furiously in my best effort to keep my head above the water. Tiva stood on the boat observing me struggle. If only my hands weren't bound together I would've been able to swim. Water started to seep into my mouth when 'Tiva stepped closer to the edge of the boat with her gun cocked and ready. Before I knew it, a loud bang filled the air and everything went black.

Na'Tiva

I watched as Na'Tya's body laid limp in the water. Instead of being sad that my little sister was gone, I felt a sense of relief that I didn't have to worry about her fucking me over anymore. Just as she told me while I was tied up in that room with her and B-Moore, my sister died a long time ago. This woman that laid in the water before me was just another bitch on the street that fucked with the wrong bitch!

She wanted to play this little twisted-ass game with me, thinking she was gonna win, and looked how she turned out? All I could do was laugh hysterically at the thought.

"What now bitch? All I was good for was just talkin' shit huh? Now look at yo' dumb ass. Good riddance bitch," I yelled out to her dead corpse.

My henchmen sat there staring at me like I had two heads. When I shot back a dirty glance at them, they quickly straightened up their faces, in fear that I'd kill them on the spot.

I turned back and gazed at Na'Tya once again, for the last time.

"Alright, let's go...Now!" I commanded.

"Yes boss," my men said in unison as the driver started up the boat and headed back to our beach house on the other side of the ocean while our other member brought the car back to the estate. Everything was planned out and executed smoothly. Now it was time to make sure that nigga B-Moore got what was coming for him.

Chapter Ten

Months passed after my incident with Na'Tya and there was no sight of B-Moore. It was as if the nigga disappeared into thin air. Gunz and his team relentlessly worked hard to find him. They checked every state to no avail. As a result, I had to take a piece of Javel's advice and plan for my future. Not only for just me, but for the baby that I was now carrying. Day after day, I grew anxious since I was lost on the fact of who the father was.

The same night I killed 'Tya, I rushed over to Gunz's to tell him about what I did, and we ended up making love right on his living room floor. Since it was so close to the time I fucked Javel in his penthouse, I'd have to wait until the baby was born to find out the truth.

The love that I had for Gunz was different than the love I'd been gaining for Javel. Gunz and I had shared more life experiences and trauma together, whereas the experiences that Javel and I had together had been pure bliss and happiness. He was a real man who was about his business, who could provide for me and the child and treat me like a queen. Javel still had his drug empire but was so good at cutting any ties to him that he was known for his many businesses that were a billion dollar conglomerate. We would never have to worry about money, clean or dirty, and our children could have a chance at living a life that we never had. They would come out of the womb into money and success, not poverty and pain.

While Gunz was a real ass nigga. He held it down for me and would do whatever that needed to be done. He was loyal, he was gritty, and he was not one to be fucked with. He didn't have time nor any desire to be a "boss," which so many strived for. He wanted to make his money and live his life. All he wanted out of life was love and to be able to have a son. He appreciated the simple things in life, due to his many near-death experiences, just like me. And for that, Gunz had me on a deep, emotional level. He was more than just a lover or a friend. I loved him like he was a part of me. But my heart and brain had two different intentions. My body yearned for both men, but my heart was with Gunz while my mind was set on Javel and our future together and building an empire for me and our family. I was conflicted and I didn't know what to do, or who to choose.

The thoughts steadily haunted me day after day. Yet today, these thoughts took a toll on me as I began to cry. I didn't want to lose Gunz, and I didn't want to lose Javel. What the fuck was I gonna do? What if the baby was Javel's? Would Gunz be hurt by that? Then again, what if the baby was Gunz's? If Javel found out that me and Gunz have been fucking on the low this whole time, he would kill Gunz. Shit, he might kill me too!

I wiped the tears from my eyes as I looked at the incoming text that came from Javel, telling me that he would be back today from his business trip. Due to his many businesses, Javel left two months ago to handle his business dealings while I stayed down here with Gunz and the goons. Luckily for me, Javel's absence allowed me to prolong my complex plan in telling him that I was pregnant. Gunz on the other hand, he knew as soon as he walked in on me throwing up in the bathroom.

"You ain't gotta lie to me ma. I know you pregnant," was the first thing that Gunz said to me that day.

"I know you caught up between me and Javel, ma. But we gotta worry about merkin' B-Moore first. When the baby comes, that's when we will deal with that shit aiight?" he instructed, and there

was not another exchange about the baby since then.

Gunz continued on as if I wasn't even pregnant. He just made sure to keep one of the men close to me for protection, since you never know if B-Moore constructed a plan against me. That was one thing I loved about Gunz, he made sure to take care of a bitch even while he was gettin' shit done.

I let out a deep sigh as I rolled out of the bed. Other than my possible baby daddy issue, things were going ok. Gunz was still on the search for B-Moore, 'Tya was out of the picture, and I was living the good life so far in Miami.

To ease the stress that had been building up today, I decided to go get some retail therapy. After taking a warm shower, I slipped into my royal blue maxi dress and matching Valentino bow-styled sandals. I pulled my hair into a high bun before grabbing my designer bag and heading out the door.

"Where to, Ms. Davis?" Rodney, my personal driver, asked while holding the car door open for me.

"To the nearby mall," I proclaimed, as I slipped into the back of the Rolls Royce Phantom.

"Yes ma'am," he simply stated before closing the door and heading back to the driver's side. I sat back and enjoyed the landscape view as we drove to our destination.

Once we got to the mall, I didn't even hesitate to shop 'til I dropped. I didn't feel the need to have my driver follow me around the mall like a little puppy, so I told him to stay in the car or at the food court 'til I was ready to go.

After hours of shopping, I was ready to head back to the condo and relax. As I trailed out of BEBE, I called Rodney, letting him know that I was ready to go.

"Alright ma'am, I'll be at the car," he reassured before we hung up.

I exited the mall and headed to the parking lot to see Rodney standing in front of the car farther down. Once I approached him I immediately handed him my bags.

"Here you go.... I might've overdid it." I smiled.

A smile spread over his chocolate face as he grabbed my bags. "A lady like yourself can never overdo it."

"You got that right Rodney." I laughed as I headed over to the car door.

Before I could wrap my hand around the door handle, I felt the cold barrel of a gun against the back of my head.

"Don't fuckin' move hoe!" The male voice echoed in my ears. Fear gripped me as I immediately caught a flashback of when me and Danielle went through this in the past.

"What the fuck!" I heard Rodney yell out.

"Shut the fuck up nigga!" I heard another man yell out.

Within minutes, the accomplice instructed Rodney to move next to me and face the car. Through the glass of the window, I could see the reflection of the men holding us hostage. There were three men in black ski masks with their guns aimed at us.

My eyes met with Rodney's and it was something in his eyes that showed me that he didn't have no fear. Without a thought, he moved his hand to his pocket in an attempt to grab his gun. Before he could successfully get his gun, the loud ring filled the air and I watched in horror as Rodney's body slumped to the ground.

"Didn't I tell yo' ass not to fuckin' move!" one of the men said as he put another bullet through Rodney's skull.

I couldn't help but scream in response. I felt so helpless as I stood there and watched Rodney die in cold blood.

"Shut the fuck up bitch!" said the man with his gun still stationed against my skull.

In one swift motion, the accomplice grabbed me, opened up the car door, and shoved me in. Not only did they shove me in the car, they shoved Rodney's dead corpse in the car too! Two of the members hopped in the driver and passenger seats, starting up the car. I screamed and screamed until the third member hopped in the back with me and hit me in the head with the butt of his gun. In an instant, my world went black.

~~~

Bright lights burned my eyes as someone pulled the black bag from off my head. I looked around trying to figure out where I was when I heard a familiar tune being whistled. In my best effort to move, I realized that I was tied to a chair once again. While I was looking around franticly, there he stood. The Reaper stood in front of me with a wicked grin on his face.

"What's good 'Tiva?" he said mockingly.

"Let me go!" I commanded as I struggled in my seat.

"Calm down baby, the party is just beginning! Plus I brought you a friend to keep you company," he announced as he motioned for one of his goons to come forward. A big burly nigga walked into the open room with what looked like a dead body draped over his shoulder. Dropping the body onto the floor, there laid a bloody and beaten B-Moore, who was also tied up.

"What the fuck! What the fuck did you do?" I screeched.

"Shit, you should have been killed this nigga, but you was taking your sweet time. So I figured I'd step in and do what you couldn't. But no need to worry, he still breathin'," the Reaper said as he kicked B-

Moore's body, causing B-Moore to groan in pain. Finally coming back to full consciousness, B-Moore looked around frantically before trying to lift up his head. Before he could fully lift his head up, the Reaper stepped on his head, slamming it back to the floor. With his foot still planted on B-Moore's head, the Reaper spoke while slowly grinding his foot farther into his head.

"I wouldn't do that if I was you," he warned B-Moore.

"Nigga what the fuck you want with me?" B-Moore yelled out in pain.

"Oh, you forgot nigga? Guess that money got to yo' head and made you forget who's work got you there," the Reaper said calmly before looking at me and smiled.

"This scene right now seems kinda familiar don't it 'Tiva?" he asked.

"I don't know what you talking about," I said, averting my eyes.

"Come on, you remember what happened with you and Danielle. Matter of fact, how about we play that game again," he said while pulling out his gun and clicking a round into the chamber.

"Which one of ya'll is going to die? Is it you, or is it you 'Tiva?" He laughed while pointing his gun at B-Moore and then back to me.

"Look, I ain't got shit to do with what you and 'Tiva got going on. Just let me go man," B-Moore pleaded.

"B-Moore you bitch nigga! You just going to throw me under the bus like that! The Reaper should kill yo' bitch ass on sight for acting like a bitch!" I spat in rage.

"You both got a point there," the Reaper chimed in while laughing hysterically.

"Man, fuck it! Do what you want, cause you're going to do that anyways," I said, sounding defeated. Closing my eyes, I decided to accept my fate when shots rang out in the building.

Quickly opening my eyes, I saw a puddle of blood forming around B-Moore's head from the two gunshot wounds that were inflicted by the Reaper. Clinking another round into the chamber, the Reaper made his way over to me, grabbing my face and shoving the gun into my mouth. Tears filled my eyes and started to stream down my face as I tried to move my head to get the gun out my mouth, but the Reaper's grip was too strong.

"Guess I lied.... Tonight isn't about to be like last time. Both of ya'll snake mothafuckas was going to die tonight!" he said with gleam.

I squinted my eyes in anticipation of the Reaper's next move. His finger seemed to move in slow motion as it wrapped around the trigger. Suddenly shots rang out in the building. I flinched in the expectation to feel pain, but instead the Reaper's body jerked violently, sending him flying to the ground.

Gunz

"Bust this left right here!" Javel instructed.

I sped down the highway, heading to the location where 'Tiva was supposed to be at. We were able to find her location due to the tracking device in her driver's cell phone. They must have been moving quickly since they forgot to dump the phone. Parking the car a few feet away from the building, I killed the light. Strapping up, I took point as we made our way to the building.

As I crept up the stairs, I noticed that the door was slightly open, enough for me to see the Reaper with his gun in 'Tiva's mouth. Not even thinking of the outcome, I pulled the trigger, sending the whole clip into the Reaper's body. Rushing in with Javel on my tail, we started to untie 'Tiva.

"You ok?" I asked while untying her feet that were strapped to the chair. All she could do was weep as Javel untied her arms. Hopping out of the seat, Tiva rushed and hugged Javel tightly. But the reunion was cut short when I heard a loud groan. Turning around, I could see the Reaper now in a sitting position looking at me enraged. I stood up quickly and pushed 'Tiva and Javel out of the way as the Reaper pulled the trigger of his gun. Bullets sprayed everywhere, hitting me in the chest, sending me flying to the ground. A burning sensation filled my body as I laid on the cold, cement ground.

Na'Tiva

Gunz laid on the ground bleeding as Javel shot back at the Reaper, hitting him a couple of times before he fell back onto the floor. When the coast was clear I dove to the ground, scooping Gunz into my arms, putting my hand over his gunshot wounds in my best effort to stop the bleeding. Gunz took my hand and shook his head. Blood seeped from his mouth as he choked, trying to speak.

"Shush, don't try to speak. Just hold on..." I pleaded with tears streaming down my face. He looked up at me and smiled while stroking the side of my face before speaking.

"I wish...I wish I would have been able to give you the life you deserved.... I love you, 'Tiva" he choked out. Within seconds, Gunz's body went still and I knew he was gone. I sat there holding him and cried. Why did he have to go? He didn't have to die, not like this!

"Come on 'Tiva, we got to go," Javel urged as he tugged at my arm.

"No! I ain't leaving him like this," I argued. Yet the sound of many footsteps coming from outside of the building grabbed my attention. The Reaper's goons must have noticed something was going on.

One of his henchmen popped into the building and Javel shot him before he could even get a shot off. But it seemed like the niggas coming into the building were never ending. Javel tried his best to keep them at bay but suffered a gunshot wound in the leg.

"Get the fuck up 'Tiva, we got to go," he yelled, this time in a commanding tone.

Full of regret, I got up and took Javel's gun to give us some cover fire while assisting him out of the building. Once we made it out, we dashed into the parking lot toward our car.

As soon as I hopped into the passenger seat, Javel sped off without looking back. Looking out the window, I cried silently to myself, in disbelief that we just left Gunz's body there. Javel reached over and tried to comfort me, but there was nothing he could do to take this pain away.

Within minutes, we pulled up to one of Javel's private doctor's offices. There waiting outside the building was the doctor with some of his nurses. They rushed to the car and helped us inside where they treated all of our wounds. But nothing could fix the broken heart that I suffered.

Epilogue

The warm sun beamed on my brown skin as I sat on the beach in Jamaica and enjoyed the view. It had been weeks since my encounter with Reaper, and it felt good to be able to get away from it all.

"Here you go," Javel said as he approached me with my coconut water.

"For you and for our child." He smiled as he sat next to me and placed his hand on my stomach.

I finally told him that I was pregnant while we were out here at our private villa, and I decided that I would make the best of my life with Javel. Gunz would forever be the one to have my heart, but I had to make a player decision and do what I had to do for my future. I didn't want to have to choose between the two, but life didn't give me no other choice. So here I was, getting ready to embark on my new life with Javel.

While Javel was taking care of his legitimate businesses, we agreed that I would help him run his drug empire. I went from working for him to working with him as his life partner.

I sat back in my beach chair and admired the twelve-carat diamond engagement ring that was wrapped around my finger. After all the hell I'd been through, I finally got what I wanted. I was the last woman standing, and now I was ruling the streets as the connect.

Excitement surged through my body. Once I got back to the states, things were bound to change. As for now, I was going to enjoy this peace and tranquility, something I hadn't had for years.

Meanwhile...

"Just hang on...you're gonna make it," was the last thing I heard as I laid on the stretcher while the ER team rushed me into my room. As they transferred me off the stretcher to the bed in the surgery room, I closed my eyes as I slipped into a deep sleep.

Once I finally woke up, I found myself in a hospital bed. I looked around only to see my man Ray sitting next to me.

"What the fuck you doin' here?" I asked as I sat up.

"I had to check up on you boss," Ray answered, looking down.

I nodded my head. "Aiight. How long I been in here for?" I interrogated.

"For three weeks boss," he replied.

"Damn," was all I could say. Vivid thoughts of what happened up in the abandoned building flashed through my mind.

"Where 'Tiva and that fuck nigga at?" I spat.

"We been keeping tabs on 'em. Last time we checked they was out in Jamaica, but word is they coming back to the states," Ray informed.

A smile began to spread across my face. They thought that a nigga was dead, but here I was. When 'Tiva get back to the states, I'll make sure I pay her a visit. She needs to know that you can't just fuck over the Reaper and get away with it.

~~~

Find out what happens next in part four of I Am The Streets! Available Now!

Your Free Chapter of Bred To Kill by Simone Majors:

Prologue

That hot, sticky summer would be the summer I would never forget. That day started like any other, with me sitting on the porch watching the kids run in and out of the broken fire hydrant, while the aroma of blazing grills filled the air. All the dope boys were out in their latest summer gear, showing off their new customize whips. But out of all the dope boys on the block, my brother shined the brightest.

King was his name, but everyone knew him as the king of the East Side. He was the envy of all the movers and shakers of Detroit, and the object of every girl's lust. King was 6'4 with smooth, cinnamon sugar skin.

His eyes were the brightest tint of hazel I had ever seen. But what really brought the girls to their knees was his smile. King had the perfect Colgate-white smile with deep dimples to match.

Still seated on the porch, I watched my brother as he sat on the hood of his all-black, old-school Impala. Dressed to impress, King wore his all-white, V-cut tee with dark blue, True Religion jeans. He rocked the hottest new pair of black and white J's, which complimented his diamond-face Rolex and Cartier frames.

As King sat there laughing and talking to his squad of friends, I noticed what looked like a black car creeping down the street. I stood up on the porch and yelled out to King, but by that time it was too late.

Gun shots filled the whole block, sounding like crackles of fireworks. I ducked down on the porch, covering my head until the sounds of squealing tires and screams no longer filled the air. Hopping up and running off the porch, I saw the sight that will forever be etched into my memory. There sprawled out on his car, King lay lifeless as blood dripped off the hood of his now shot-up Impala.

On that hot, sticky summer day, on the Detroit east side, someone took my brother away from me. They killed him in cold blood in front of his own home! On his own block!

On that hot, sticky summer day, I realized how cold the D could really be...

Chapter 1

Introducing Queen

It had been two years since my brother's murder, and here I was still on the fucked up east side. His death was the mark of a change in eras. New and upcoming dope dealers swarmed the east side, taking over my brother's blocks. Honor of the street code was now a thing of the past.

Shit, even loyalty was hard to come by now. The most loyal person I have ever known was King. When my mother lost her job at the Chrysler plant, due to getting laid off, King didn't think twice about hitting the streets. He put his ass on the line daily to make sure my mom and I ate. We was what you could call hood rich. No longer bound to working at the plant, my mother, Loni, decided that she was going to take full advantage of the lifestyle her son had blessed her with.

You could always catch my mom at the casino, bars, and nightclubs any day of the week. But despite that, I never felt any way about her being out so much, because I had King. He was the one that made sure I did my homework every day without fail. Every night before he left to handle business, he made sure I was tucked in and safe. And by the time the sunlight peek through my window, he was downstairs whipping up breakfast to make sure I didn't go to school hungry.

I guess you could say that King was more like a parent then a brother to me. But with his untimely death, my mother was devastated by how we was going to keep up our hood-rich lifestyle. So me getting a job was the first thing on her list.

Standing in the mirror, I looked at my thick 5'2 frame, dressed in my Popeye's chicken uniform. Mann this wack-ass uniform didn't do me any justice! The horrible, orange oversized shirt made me look like an Oompa Loompa, when in reality I had smooth, caramel skin. Fingering through my short brown hair that was styled into a cute bob, I placed the Popeye's chicken visor on my head and walked out of my room.

My mother sat on the couch with the air conditioning blowing, watching TV before she turned to speak.

"What time you getting off today?" she said as she looked me up and down.

"Around ten I think?" I responded while slipping on my black shoes for crews made personally for fast food workers.

"Don't you get paid today? Shit, I need some money to pay this fucking light bill!" my mother announced as she got off the couch, walking in my direction.

"Well I can't do shit about that! Maybe if you got yo ass up and tried to get a job, then you wouldn't be worried about the light bill needing to be paid!" I spat.

"What the fuck you think I look like working!" my mother scoffed as she folded her arms in dismay.

"You look like a mother trying to take care of her fucking household!" I said as I rolled my eyes.

"A bitch like me don't have to work! When King was here he made sure I lived right!"

"Well I ain't King, and I will not be putting my life on the line just for yo ass to live the hood-rich life! So I guess you have to figure that light bill situation out yo self!" I yelled before grabbing my purse and heading out the front door.

I marched down the street toward the bus stop, fuming at the fact that my mother's lazy ass didn't feel the need to take care of her household. To be honest, I didn't even understand how my brother dealt with her stupid ass. After standing at the bus stop for a couple of minutes, I saw the bus coming down the street. I sighed as the bus stopped in front of me. *Another day at the hell house,* I thought as I boarded the bus and made my way to work.

~~~

When I made it back home, it was way after ten, but one thing I did notice when I walked up the porch steps was that our lights were still on.

Thanking God that my mother finally listened to what I said, I walked into the house only to see her cuddled up on the couch with some old-school ass nigga.

"Momma, who the fuck you got up in this house, lying up with you?"

"Queen, stop being disrespectful. This my little friend Benny. You remember Benny?"

"No the fuck I don't, and that still doesn't answer the question why he up in our house!"

"Well miss rudeness, if you must know, Benny was kind enough to pay the light bill, since yo ass didn't want to help yo momma out!"

"So instead of getting yo fucking ass a job, you decided to go out and find a nigga to pay it for you?"

"Queen, I'm not bout to have you disrespecting my company, just because yo selfish ass didn't want to help out around here!"

"So what did you have to do, to get him to pay yo light bill, Momma?"

"Look here, little girl, mind yo business!" my mother said sternly before shooing me off. I rolled my eyes and stomped up the stairs. Everyone in the hood knew Benny no good ass! Benny was one of the old heads in the hood who still was on top of his game. He was known to have the purest of coke and a brothel full of hoes on his team.

Everyone knew not to get involved with his grimy ass, because when you owed him money, he made sure you paid him and then some. The fact that my mother would stoop so low, to get into bed with this nigga, made me sick! Making it to my room, I gathered up my things to take a shower.

Once in the shower, I scrubbed any trace of Popeye's chicken from my skin. After getting fresh and clean, I was walking back to my room when I heard loud moaning and groaning coming from my mother's room downstairs. I shook my head in disgust and walked into my room and slammed the door.

Turning on my radio and blasting some music, I tuned my mother and her shenanigans out. I laid back on my bed and grabbed my picture frame with a photo of me and my brother at my eighth grade farewell. A tear slowly formed in my eye thinking about how two years had flown by so quickly.

But there hasn't been a day that I haven't missed him. If King were here right now, I knew that he wouldn't let mom talk to Benny's lame ass. Shit, Benny wouldn't have been able to step foot in this house if King were here. I rolled over and placed the picture frame back on my nightstand and tried to get me some sleep.

Get Your Copy of Bred To Kill Today!